GERALD McDERMOTT

MUSICIANS OF THE SUN

SIMON & SCHUSTER BOOKS FOR YOUNG READERS

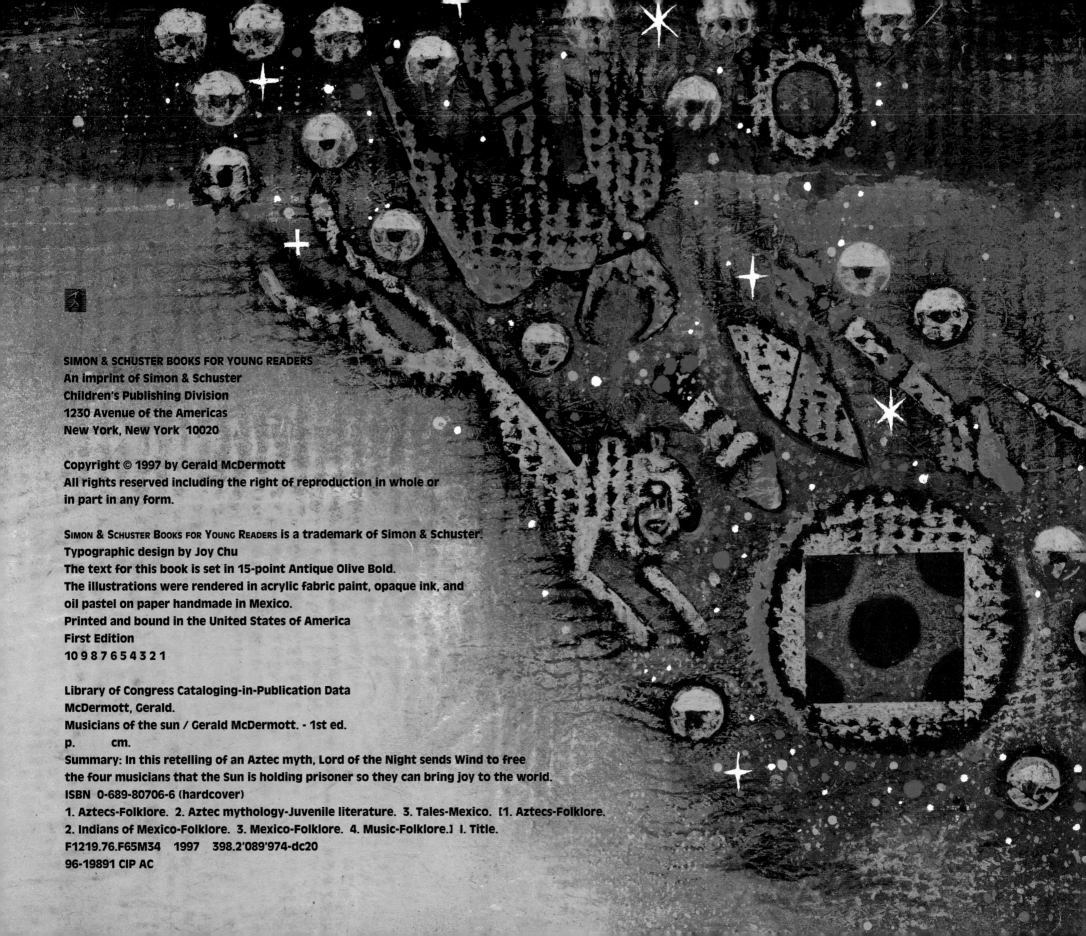

SIMON & SCHUSTER BOOKS FOR YOUNG READERS
An imprint of Simon & Schuster
Children's Publishing Division
1230 Avenue of the Americas
New York, New York 10020

SIMON & SCHUSTER BOOKS FOR YOUNG READERS is a trademark of Simon & Schuster.
Typographic design by Joy Chu
The text for this book is set in 15-point Antique Olive Bold.
The illustrations were rendered in acrylic fabric paint, opaque ink, and
oil pastel on paper handmade in Mexico.
Printed and bound in the United States of America
First Edition
10 9 8 7 6 5 4 3 2 1

Library of Congress Cataloging-in-Publication Data
McDermott, Gerald.
Musicians of the sun / Gerald McDermott. - 1st ed.
p.   cm.
Summary: In this retelling of an Aztec myth, Lord of the Night sends Wind to free
the four musicians that the Sun is holding prisoner so they can bring joy to the world.
ISBN 0-689-80706-6 (hardcover)
1. Aztecs-Folklore. 2. Aztec mythology-Juvenile literature. 3. Tales-Mexico. [1. Aztecs-Folklore.
2. Indians of Mexico-Folklore. 3. Mexico-Folklore. 4. Music-Folklore.] I. Title.
F1219.76.F65M34   1997   398.2'089'974-dc20
96-19891 CIP AC

For Julia

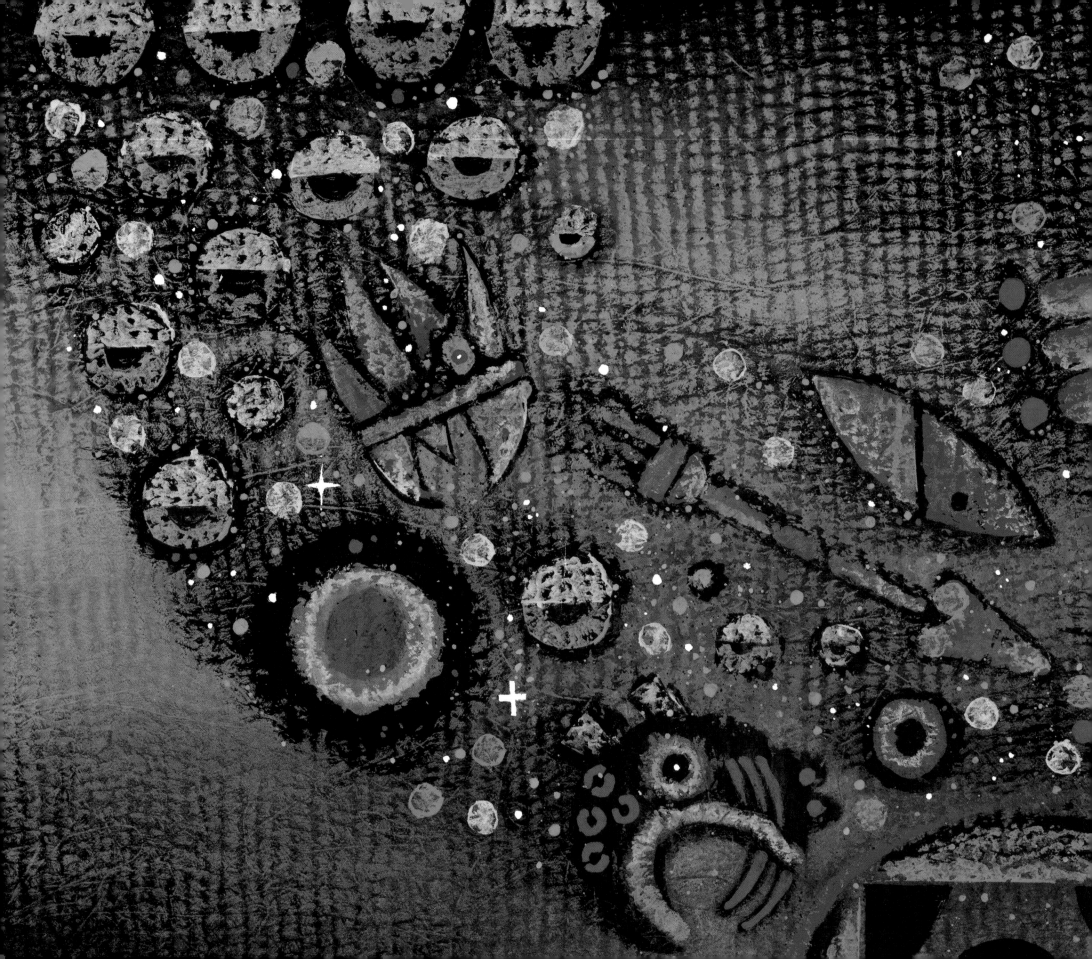

Out of the starry night he came,
invisible,
untouchable.

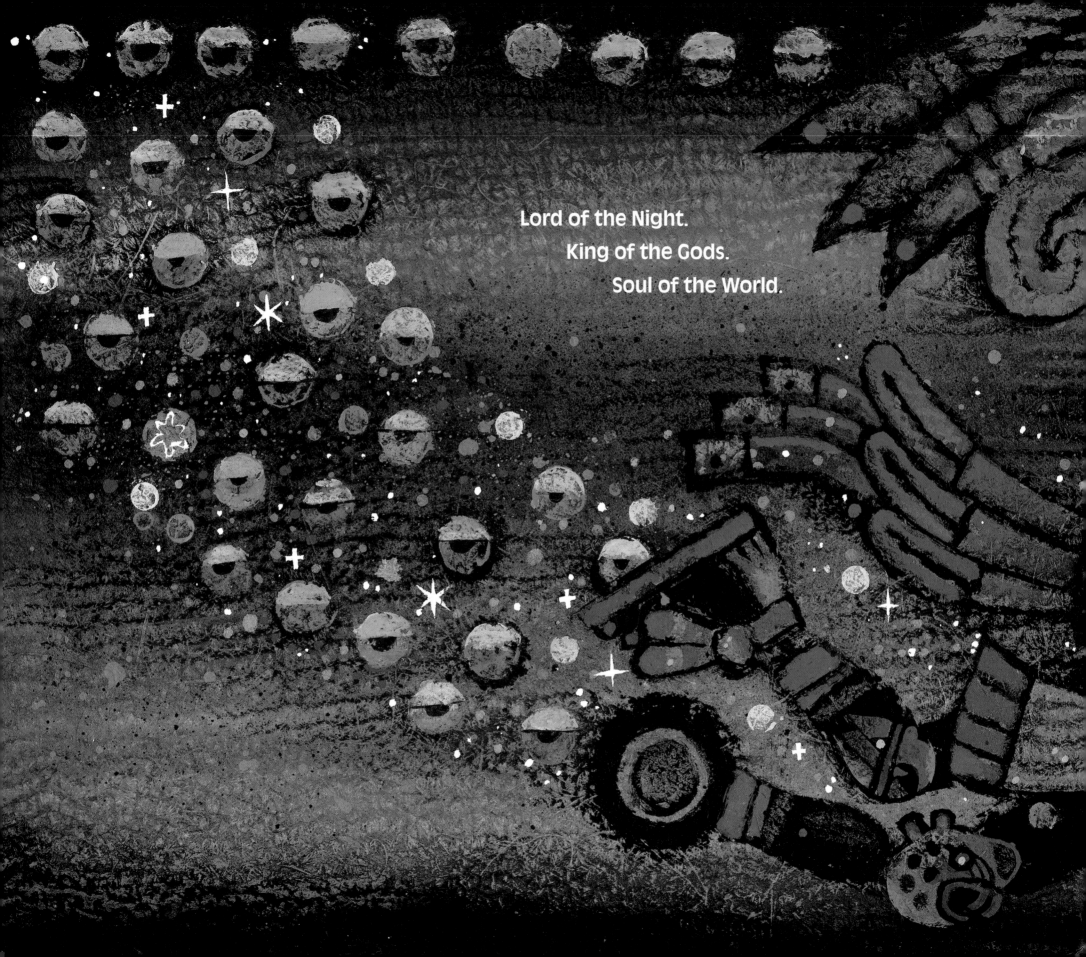

Lord of the Night.
King of the Gods.
Soul of the World.

Lord of the Night
had a magic mirror.
It was his third eye.
In it he could see all Earth.
"The world is gray and joyless,"
he said.

" Children do not laugh.
Women do not dance.
Men do not sing.
The people spend their lives
in darkness and silence.
I will change all this,"
declared Lord of the Night.

Lord of the Night called Wind to his side.
"O Wind," he said, "fly to the house of the Sun.
Free the four musicians held prisoner there:
Red, Yellow, Blue, and Green.
Bring them to Earth so the people
may hear their music."

" But, Lord," said Wind, "Sun is a mighty warrior
who destroys his enemies with fire. I am nothing
but air. How will I overcome his power?"
" Do not be afraid," said Lord of the Night.
" I will arm you."

Lord of the Night gave Wind a turquoise shield,
a black thundercloud, and shining silver lightning.
Wind took the weapons and swept across the
mountains, searching for the house of the Sun.

At last he reached the edge of the sea.
He met Turtle Woman, Fish Woman and
Alligator Woman on the shore.
" Where is the house of the Sun?" asked Wind.
" On the other side of the sea," answered Turtle Woman.
" Too far for Wind to blow."

" It is a long journey over waves and through
  darkness," said Fish Woman. "Your strength will fail."
" But Lord of the Night has sent me," said Wind.
" I must free the prisoners of the Sun."

"We will help you," said Alligator Woman.

Turtle Woman, Fish Woman and Alligator Woman carried
Wind far across the sea.
The sky began to glow.
"Faster!" cried Wind. "Before Sun rises too high."
The three women swam until the
sea foamed white behind them.

Now Sun was shining above the horizon.
Wind took a great breath and leaped into the sky.
As he flew up toward the house of the Sun
he heard the sweet music of flute, drum,
shell, and rattle.
"Musicians of the Sun," called Wind,
"I am coming to free you!"

The musicians heard the voice of Wind.
They yearned to be free,
but Sun made them more fearful.
They continued to play.
"Go away!" said Sun to Wind.
"Or I will destroy you."

Wind went closer still and called out again,
"Musicians of the Sun, come with me!"
"Ignore him," said Sun. "Play on."
Sun burned more fiercely, and
the musicians played louder
than before.

Wind came near.
"Musicians of the Sun, I am here to
take you down to Earth!"
"Come no closer!" Sun shouted.
He hurled a rain of fire-darts at Wind.
Wind raised his turquoise shield
and was not harmed.

Then Wind howled and unleashed his thunder.
Black clouds spilled forth. Darkness
covered the face of Sun, and his light
grew dim.

The four musicians huddled together.
"We are frightened, O Wind!" they cried.
"Then come with me to Earth," said Wind.
"I promise you freedom."

The musicians grasped Wind's cloak
as he leaped away from the house of the Sun.
Wind threw his shining silver lightning
to cut through the darkness below.

"Come back," bellowed Sun. "I command you!"
But Sun was lost in the black clouds
and he was powerless.

Wind carried the musicians through the sky,
across the stars, and gently down to Earth.
Lord of the Night welcomed them.
"Play your music," he said. "Bring happiness
to my people."

The musicians curled their toes in the cool earth and began to play.

Red faced east and played a song of joy on her drum.

Yellow faced west and played a lullaby on his flute.

Blue faced south and played a song of night on her shell. Green faced north and played a song of dawn on his rattles.

Wind carried the beautiful sounds around Earth.

The world filled with color.

Children laughed.

Women danced.

Men sang.

Even Sun was happy

and poured out his light

upon them.

All gave thanks to
Lord of the Night.
King of the Gods.
Soul of the World.

A Note About the Story

Musicians of the Sun is a lost fragment of the mythological tradition of the Aztecs, the powerful warrior society that dominated central Mexico from the fourteenth to the sixteenth centuries. When the Spanish conquistadors arrived in 1519, they subjugated the Aztecs, pulled down their temples and used the stones for the foundations of churches and government buildings. They burned almost all the precious bark-paper manuscripts that recorded, in picture-writing, Aztec customs, history, and religion.

Soon after, missionary friars began a belated effort to preserve the oral traditions of the surviving Aztec storytellers. The present tale was first set down in the sixteenth century by Fray Andrés de Olmos. Although his original manuscript was lost, the text survived in a French translation, *Histoyre du Mechique* (1543). Variations of the tale also appeared in the *Historia eclesiástica indiana*, Lib. II, Cap. III, of Gerónimo de Mendieta, (1596), and the *Monarquia indiana*, Lib. VI, Cap. XLIII, of Juan de Torquemada (1615).

My redaction of this ancient tale is animated by the principal Aztec deity, Tezcatlipoca, Lord of the Night. His name means "Smoking Mirror," for the clouded disc of volcanic glass in which he can see all things. Lord of the Night emerges out of a dark sky dotted with "eyes of the night," the circular Aztec glyph for stars. He is accompanied by an owl who symbolizes his nocturnal nature.

The Lord of the Night summons the wind god, Ecehatl. Wind wears a bird beak mask through which he blows, and he is adorned with a "wind jewel," the spiky cross-section of a conch shell. He must battle with Sun, the mighty Tonatiuh, in order to bring music and color to earth.

During the years it took to bring this work to completion, the story became for me a metaphor for the artist's journey.

I rendered the illustrations for the book in acrylic fabric paint, opaque ink, and oil pastel on paper handmade in Mexico.

— G.M.